Sandy Lane Stables

Sandy Lane Stables

Riding Holiday

Michelle Bates

Adapted by Caroline Young

Reading consultant: Alison Kelly

Series editor: Lesley Sims

Designed by Brenda Cole

Cover and inside illustrations: Barbara Bongini

Map illustrations: John Woodcock

This edition first published in 2016 by Usborne Publishing Ltd.,
Usborne House, 83-85 Saffron Hill, London EC1N 8RT, England.
www.usborne.com

Contents

1.	Sandy Lane Stables	7
2.	They're Off!	15
3.	A Strange Beginning	22
4.	Graytops Horse Farm	29
5.	The Hard Work Begins	37
6.	A Surprising Visitor	44
7.	An Old Friend	52
8.	A Revelation and a Decision	61
9.	An Unusual Offer	71
10.	Stakeout	77
11.	Trouble	85
12.	Drastic Measures	94
13.	Night Watch	99
14.	Clevedon Park	104
15.	A Nasty Discovery	113
16.	All is Revealed	121

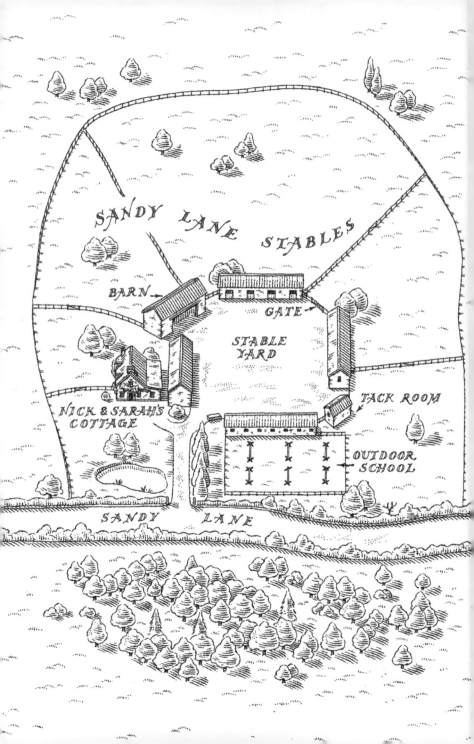

Chapter 1

Sandy Lane Stables

Izzy Paterson stood in the middle of the yard at Sandy Lane, grinning from ear to ear. "I can't believe we're actually going – a three week holiday in the States, with all the riding we could want!"

"I know," said her friend Kate eagerly. "It's going to be the holiday of a lifetime."

Everyone at Sandy Lane had been so excited when Nick and Sarah Brooks, the stable owners, had announced the prize for the Sandy Lane Christmas raffle: a two week riding holiday in the States. Now, in just one week, Izzy and Kate would be boarding the plane.

The holiday of a lifetime... The words rang in Izzy's ears. Sarah had told them that where they'd be staying – the Graytops Farm for racehorses – was amazing. She'd known the owners, Doug and Sally Bryant, since childhood, and was godmother to their twin daughters, Megan and Courtney. Izzy and Kate were going to live and ride with the family and, in return, the twins would come back to Sandy Lane next summer. For Izzy, everything was perfect – except for one, very important, thing.

"Izzy, what's the matter?" Kate asked, noticing a sad look on her friend's face.

"It's nothing," Izzy said. "It's just… well, if only I didn't have to leave Midnight." She turned to stroke the sleek, black horse beside her.

"Oh Izzy, you know we can't take him with us."

"I know." Izzy sighed. "But I didn't realize how bad I'd feel when I was actually faced with leaving him behind."

"He'll be in good hands here at Sandy Lane," Kate

reassured her. "And three weeks will fly by. Before you know it, we'll be back."

"You're right," said Izzy, a little more cheerfully. "And Rosie's agreed to ride him at the Colcott Show next weekend, so he won't miss out."

"You couldn't *not* go on this trip," Kate said with a smile. "Hey, look who's coming over, right on cue."

Izzy glanced across the yard, and saw Rosie coming out of the tack room, a bridle slung over her shoulder and a saddle, crop, riding hat and numerous brushes gathered in her arms.

"I give it ten seconds before she drops something," said Izzy, chuckling.

"Hey, how's it going?" Rosie called as she walked towards them. "Let me guess what you're talking about – your big trip?"

"Got it in one." Kate grinned.

"I don't blame you," said Rosie. "You must be pretty excited. Do you mind if I take over grooming Midnight, Izzy? Oops!" she cried, as everything she was carrying dropped to the floor.

"Course not," Izzy answered, smirking at Kate as she helped Rosie pick the things up. "He's all yours. I've got high hopes for you and Midnight. You'll be winning the Colcott Open Jumping trophy for me."

"Well, I'll certainly do my best," said Rosie. She turned to Kate. "I hear you had another email from Courtney and Megan today. What did they say?"

Kate took her phone from her pocket. "I'll read it out while you're tacking up, in my best American accent," she announced, taking a deep breath.

"Hey you guys, how's it going over there? It's been pretty crazy at school with our finals and stuff..."

"Well, you can skip the boring bits," said Izzy.

Kate giggled, and carried on reading. *"The farm looks awesome. We've been taking Garnet and Prince—"*

"Their ponies," Izzy interrupted, leaning over Kate's shoulder.

"Are you going to let me read this?" asked Kate indignantly. Izzy poked out her tongue at her but Kate had gone back to the email. *"We've been taking Garnet and Prince to the creek to swim, but they don't* really do much more than wade because Garnet is afraid of the water and Prince won't do anything by himself. It's crazy busy on the farm right now, with all the race meets coming up. We'll fill you in on everything when you get here. You're probably more interested in hearing about all the riding you'll be doing anyway. Don't worry, there'll be plenty of that! We'll have to take turns riding Garnet and Prince, but Mom has been talking to Nick and she seems to think you'll be working some of the racehorses too."

"That's so cool," Izzy said excitedly. "We'll be riding real racehorses."

"That's all we've got time for now, guys," Kate continued. "So we'll see you both on the 2nd. Can't wait to meet you. Love, Courtney and Megan."

"It does sound wonderful," said Rosie, wistfully. "I'd be even more jealous if it wasn't for the Colcott Show and riding Midnight."

"Talking of the Show..." said Kate. "See who's here now." The girls looked across the yard to see Tom Buchanan striding over.

"Uh oh, I'd better get a move on," Rosie said.

"Don't panic." Izzy grabbed her arm. "Tom doesn't run the stables, you know."

"Are you sure about that?" Kate muttered.

Tom was the star rider at Sandy Lane and had recently taken charge of all the jumping practice for the summer shows. It took some of the pressure off Nick and was good experience for Tom, who was training to be a riding instructor.

"Hey you lot... haven't you got anything better to do than stand around gossiping?" Tom snapped.

"Here we go again," muttered Kate.

"Jumping practice is in ten minutes, Rosie," he reminded her as he walked away.

"Don't worry, I'll be there." Rosie looked at Izzy and raised her eyebrows. "I guess I'd better get a move on."

"You should go when you're ready to go, Rosie," Izzy said.

"I know, but winding Tom up isn't worth it."

"Did you hear what I said, Rosie? Ten minutes."

Tom had come back. "By the way, Izzy... Kate... I'm afraid there isn't room for you in today's practice."

"What?" Izzy groaned.

"I've already got ten riders," Tom went on. "And you know Nick doesn't like me teaching any more than that."

"But—" Izzy started.

"No buts." Tom was firm. "You know the rules – the first ones to sign up get priority."

"But you must have known we'd want to join in," Kate insisted. "I mean, I know we're not competing at Colcott, but we are regular riders at Sandy Lane."

"That may be true," said Tom, with a shrug, "but it doesn't give you automatic entry to my practices." With that, he was gone.

"Of all the patronising, smug..." Izzy was fuming.

"Calm down, Izzy," Rosie said, jumping to Tom's defence. "Tom is under a lot of pressure with his instructor's exams coming up and everything."

"I suppose so," agreed Izzy, "but you have to admit that ever since he's taken up this teaching business he's been a complete nightmare."

"You can say that again." Kate sighed.

"He's been a complete nightmare," Izzy repeated with a grin.

"Ha, ha! I'm sure he'll be back to his old self soon enough," said Rosie, taking Midnight's reins.

"Let's hope so," Izzy said, giving Midnight one final pat.

The stables were busy that morning – riders dashing this way and that and horses stamping their feet in anticipation of the ride ahead.

"If you ask me, this holiday couldn't have come at a better time," Izzy commented. "If I was going to have to stay here and take lessons from Tom all summer, I'd be soooo fed up."

Kate nodded. "Me too."

"Six more days to go." Izzy sighed. "I don't know how we're going to get through them."

Chapter 2

They're Off!

To their relief, the following week sped by, and it seemed like no time at all before the girls were off to the airport, bags packed and ready.

It wasn't until they were sitting on the plane that either of them believed they were really going. The girls were both fizzing with excitement.

"What time do we get to Graytops?" Kate asked, when they were settled in their seats. "I can't wait!"

"About ten o'clock tonight," Izzy said. "That's four o'clock in the morning UK time."

"And it's a two hour drive from the airport?" said

Kate. "And the Bryants did say they'd meet us?"

"Yes... Stop worrying, Kate!" Izzy replied.

"OK. I just wanted to double-check," said Kate. "I haven't travelled as much as you have, don't forget. Hey – what do you think Graytops will be like?"

"Endless paddocks, birds soaring in a bright blue sky, days of riding in the warm sunshine, horses kicking up dust on long trails..."

"You've got a vivid imagination!" Kate laughed.

"That's what comes of having an author for a dad," said Izzy. "Wake me up when we get there!" With that, she put her seat back and closed her eyes.

"Would all passengers from flight AA123 from London Heathrow please proceed to Baggage Claim Zone B," announced a voice over the intercom.

"That's us!" said Kate.

The girls hurried over to the right conveyor belt to see suitcases, holdalls, rucksacks, bags and boxes... but not theirs.

"Isn't that them over there?" said Kate, pointing.

"Yes!" Izzy grabbed the bags and put them on a trolley. "Let's go."

"I feel like a celeb," Kate whispered, seeing the waiting faces in the Arrivals hall. "Can you see the Bryants?"

"Not yet," Izzy answered. "Wait here and I'll have a look around."

Two minutes later, she was back. "Nope, I can't see them anywhere."

"Maybe they're a bit late," Kate said.

"But what if they don't come?" Izzy looked worried. "Should we call home?"

"No, we'll call Graytops," said Kate. "Hang on a minute. Who's that?"

She had spotted a man standing by himself, holding up a sign with their names scrawled on it.

"That must be Mr. Bryant. How could we have missed him?" Kate whispered.

"Maybe because we were expecting the whole family to come and meet us," Izzy muttered. "Come on. Let's say hello."

The girls pushed their loaded luggage trolley across to the man.

"Mr. Bryant?" Kate said tentatively. "I'm Kate Hardy and this is Izzy Paterson."

"Oh, hi there, but I'm not Mr. Bryant," the man said. "I'm your taxi driver."

Kate and Izzy exchanged surprised glances.

"Oh, uh, right, we thought the Bryants were going to be picking us up," said Izzy.

"No, no, I've been asked to collect you," the driver said. "Look, here's the booking right here." He showed them his mobile, with an email from the Bryants. There was an awkward silence. "So where are you girls from?"

"England," Izzy said.

"Near London?" the man asked.

"Not exactly," said Kate.

"Let's get going, then," the taxi driver said, walking towards his car.

Izzy and Kate looked at each other.

"Do you think this is all right, Izzy?" asked Kate.

"I think it's fine, but it is a little weird... The Bryants did say they'd be here." Izzy frowned for a moment. "Anyway, I'm sure they'll explain when we get to Graytops. We could try ringing them but I've got no signal yet."

Kate shook her head. "Me neither." She looked at the waiting driver. "I think we'd better go with him, or we'll be stranded here..."

It was dark when the taxi turned off a main road and through some huge iron gates. Kate nudged Izzy, who had fallen asleep.

"Izzy... Izzy, I think we're here," she murmured.

"What?" Izzy mumbled.

"We're here," said Kate.

"Here? Where?" Izzy sat bolt upright.

"Graytops."

"Oh right." Izzy grunted. "I think I must have fallen asleep."

"You don't say." Kate laughed.

The car stopped by a large, white-painted wooden house with grey, sloping roofs.

"It's massive," Kate whispered.

"It looks so different from the houses at home, too," said Izzy.

"Here you are," the driver said, getting their bags out. As soon as the girls opened the car doors, the hot air hit them. After the cool of the air-conditioned taxi, it was like stepping into a sauna.

"It's *baking*," said Izzy.

The driver put their bags down beside them. "I'll be off now. Enjoy your vacation."

"That was some taxi," Kate said, watching the car glide away. "More like a limousine. Everything seems so much bigger out here..."

The two girls went up to the front door of the house, and rang the bell.

"It's lovely and peaceful, isn't it?" Izzy said, looking around.

Kate smiled. "Looks like we're in the middle of nowhere."

They stood, waiting, for several minutes. Finally, Izzy peeked in through the side window. "Hmm...

You know, I can't see any lights on."

"I wish they'd hurry up," Kate said. "I'm shattered."

"Me too." Izzy peered in through the window again. "I don't think there's anyone in."

"There must be," Kate said, trying the bell again.

"Maybe we should head over there...?" Izzy pointed to some lights in the distance.

They turned down a track, but the lights seemed to be getting further away rather than nearer, and it was growing darker.

"Bit scary, isn't it?" Izzy shivered.

"We'll be fine," said Kate, trying not to sound as nervous as she felt.

"I think I can hear voices." Izzy grabbed Kate by the arm. "Ahead of us... listen."

"I can't hear a thing."

"This feels wrong. It's as if we're tresp—"

A voice boomed out from behind them. "Hey, you two! What do you think you're doing?"

Izzy and Kate spun around, hearts pounding. This was not the warm welcome they had expected at all.

Chapter 3

A Strange Beginning

"Well, who are you?" the voice came again. It was a man, and he sounded pretty angry.

"We're... we're..." Kate stuttered. She stopped as the man appeared out of the darkness. He was dressed in a uniform and had a dog on a leash.

"We're K-kate Hardy and Izzy Paterson," Kate tried again. "We've come to s-s-stay."

"To stay?" The man still sounded suspicious, but less cross. The dog at his side growled menacingly.

"There's nobody home," Izzy said.

"No, they're all over at the stables," the man

answered gruffly. He lifted his hand and jerked it behind him. "Head to your right."

"Thanks!" said Kate.

"And don't go wandering off," the man shouted after them.

"Strange." Kate shivered as the man vanished into the darkness again. "I suppose he must be a security guard. You'd have thought he'd have been told we were coming."

"Yeah, I know. Hey – wait a minute." Izzy held out her arm to stop Kate.

"Why? What is it?"

"There, up ahead," Izzy said. "The voices... Can you hear them now? They don't sound happy."

"Yes," said Kate. "They sound really annoyed. And look – what are all those people doing?" She strained her eyes to see and could just make out an archway and, beyond that, a yard.

A trailer stood with its ramp down and a group of people crowded around it. A man seemed to be trying to load up a horse, while a woman next to him was struggling to grab the lead rope.

"That's weird," Kate said. "Why do you think they're transporting horses at night?"

"Perhaps they do that at racing stables," said Izzy.

"I guess so," Kate said, still unsure.

When they were within fifty paces of the lights, they stopped. The horse had been led into the box and the group of people stood, talking heatedly. Izzy and Kate could only catch snippets of the conversation.

"We wouldn't do anything like that. Give us the benefit of the doubt..."

"If you take him away now it could ruin everything..."

"We'll get to the bottom of this, I promise it'll be all right..."

"Let's go over," Kate said. "It feels wrong, eavesdropping like this."

Izzy nodded. They waited for a moment as the trailer backed through the archway, its headlights lighting up the trees, before they walked forward.

Nobody noticed them approaching at first. Then, two girls spotted them and rushed over. "Hey Mom. It's Izzy and Kate... they're here already!" said one.

"How did you get here so quickly? Are you tired? How was the flight?" asked the other, in one breath.

Izzy smiled, and looked from one girl to the other. They looked almost exactly the same.

"Sorry, I guess we'd better start by introducing ourselves." One of the girls laughed. "I'm Courtney and this is Megan."

At first glance, the girls looked identical in every way – both had long, red hair and bright green eyes – but when Izzy looked more closely, she realized that Courtney was slightly taller.

"Hi there," a woman called out. The same woman they had seen near the trailer was walking towards them. "Good to see you!" She was smiling, but she sounded exhausted. "I'm Mrs. Bryant. Call me Sally. Welcome to Graytops. I'm sorry we couldn't be there to meet you at the airport. Something... came up. You must be pretty tired. Let's get you settled in."

"Aw, Mom, Izzy and Kate'll want to look at the horses first," said Courtney.

"Tomorrow, girls." Sally laughed. "I know you're excited, but it's really late and Kate and Izzy have just come off a long-haul flight. I'm sure they'll want to get their heads down."

"I never thought I'd hear myself say I'd rather sleep than see horses!" Izzy turned to look at Kate. "But I'm so tired."

"Me too." Kate agreed.

The girls followed Sally back to the house, the twins chatting all the way about their plans for the weeks ahead.

"Here we are," said Sally, as they reached the steps of the house. "Courtney... Megan, can you bring up Izzy and Kate's bags? I'll take them up to their room."

Inside, the house was cool and the girls were glad to be out of the heat. As they climbed the wooden staircase, they noticed all the photographs on the walls. 'Seattle Surprise winning the Ashworth Maiden Stakes,' read one of them. 'Doug Bryant being presented with the bowl for best new trainer,' read another.

"Will Mr. Bryant be back soon?" Kate asked, glancing at the photos.

"Uh, well, he's not staying here right now," Sally answered vaguely. "In fact, he'll probably be away for most of your visit." They arrived at a room with two single beds in it. "Oh no, I've completely forgotten to make up your beds. How foolish of me! Would you mind doing it yourselves?"

"No, that's fine," said Izzy, trying not to sound too surprised, though her heart sank at the thought that she couldn't just fall into bed.

"Thanks," Sally said. "It's been a long day and I'm beat! If you need anything, I'm just at the end of the hall and the girls are next door. Good night and sleep well. Come on Courtney and Megan... it's bedtime for you too."

As soon as the door closed behind them, Izzy turned to Kate. "So where's Mr. Bryant?" she hissed. "Isn't it odd he won't be here at all?"

"Maybe they're having a few, you know, problems," said Kate, unfolding her duvet cover.

Izzy nodded, and started making up her own bed. "But no one even explained why a taxi met us at the airport. And why didn't Sally make up the beds earlier? My mum would never have forgotten something like that."

"Neither would mine." Kate shook out her quilt as Izzy wandered into the en suite bathroom to clean her teeth. "But Sally does seem really busy."

"True." Izzy wiped toothpaste foam from her mouth and yawned.

"And Courtney and Megan were really friendly when they saw us. I've never seen anyone look so disappointed when we said we wanted to go to bed rather than meet the horses." Kate paused. "Izzy? Didn't you think they were friendly?"

But Izzy had collapsed into bed and was already fast asleep.

Chapter 4

Graytops Horse Farm

When Kate and Izzy looked out of their bedroom window the next morning, all their niggling worries vanished. It looked wonderful – acres of white-railed paddocks stretching before their eyes, lime trees blowing in the breeze and a beautiful creek shimmering in the morning sun.

"Wow!" said Izzy. "Check that out."

"It's great." Kate smiled. "And look over there."

Izzy looked and saw a large oval-shaped paddock full of horses and riders.

"The grey mare is beautiful," said Kate.

"Isn't she?" Izzy grinned.

"That must be some kind of training track," Kate said. "Let's get down there and take a look."

The two girls showered, dressed and hurried downstairs. There was nobody about at all, which surprised them.

"What do you think we should do?" Kate asked, walking into the kitchen. "Should we help ourselves to breakfast?"

"Can you see a note or anything?"

"It's half eight already. They're probably at the yard. Let's skip breakfast and go and find them."

It had been hard for the girls to see the stables in the dark, but now, lit by the morning sun, the farm looked incredible. Two large white-washed barns stood opposite each other. There was a tack room and, at the top of the gravelled yard, a red-brick building which looked as though it might be an office. Izzy and Kate were just wondering where to go when Sally appeared from one of the barns and called across to them.

"Hi there, you two. Come on over! You've arrived at our busiest time. The exercise string has just come in from training, but don't worry, the yard will clear in a minute. Most of the riders are only here for an hour. They'll be on to the next stables after that."

"Sally... Sally!"

The two girls turned to see a man walking towards them. He was small and stocky with grey hair and a tanned, wrinkly face.

"Can you take a look at Seattle Surprise?" the man said. "She's limping."

"Oh no." Sally groaned. "That's all we need. I'll be right there. By the way, Ted, these are our guests from England, Izzy and Kate." She gestured to the girls. "Do you remember me mentioning them?"

"Oh yeah," the man mumbled, but he had walked off before Izzy and Kate had a chance to say 'hello'.

"Well, that was our stable manager, Ted Bailey," said Sally. "Don't worry if he seems unfriendly. He spends most of his time around horses, and doesn't really 'get' people. He does a great job, though, and is one hundred percent reliable – unlike some of the stable managers we've had in the past." She shook her head, sighing. "Now, why don't you go and find Courtney and Megan? They'll be in the barn over there," she finished, rushing after Ted.

"It's a lot more hectic here than Sandy Lane," said Izzy, as they walked over to the barn.

Inside, the building was divided into two rows of five stalls, with an aisle running down the middle.

"You made it!" cried a voice from the end stall.

"Are you ready for your guided tour?" a second voice asked.

"Of course!" Izzy and Kate answered in unison.

Courtney and Megan led them out of the building and across the yard.

"How many horses do you have here?" Izzy asked. "Do they all race?"

"Fifteen," Megan replied. "But some are too young to race yet."

The girls walked into the next barn. "And here are our ponies – Prince and Garnet," said Megan.

Izzy and Kate looked over each of the stalls to see two lovely-looking ponies – a chestnut with two white socks, and a big, bay pony, with fine black markings and large brown eyes.

Courtney drew back the bolt on the door and stepped into the stall. "How's it going, buddy?" she said, tickling Prince behind his ears. "We should take them out to the paddocks to graze. Kate, do you want to grab Garnet?"

Kate drew back the bolt to the chestnut's stall. Taking the lead-rope from the hook on the wall, she clipped it onto his headcollar and led him out.

Courtney and Kate walked the ponies across the gravel to the back gate. Then they let Garnet and Prince off their ropes. The ponies ambled just a few feet away, and started nibbling at the grass happily.

Courtney smiled at the ponies, and then pointed to the paddock. "Those are the new yearlings. We've taken on three in training this year."

"Look at the speed of them." Kate gasped, watching two colts and a filly kick up their heels and gallop across the grass.

Most of the horses had been taken off to be rubbed down by the time the girls turned back to the yard, so Megan and Courtney took Izzy and Kate into the next horse barn and led them down the line of racehorses, telling them each one's name, and which races they had competed in.

Izzy looked into a stall at a beautiful black stallion – sleek and polished with a long white blaze. "Hey!" She reached in to pat his neck. "How old is he? He's magnificent. Ouch!" She jumped back in surprise as the horse tried to bite a chunk out of her arm.

"You've just met Fiery Lad." Courtney chuckled. "He's kinda temperamental."

"I don't think he likes you, Izzy." Kate laughed.

"Well I like him," she said.

Kate had stopped at the backside of a grey mare and was looking her up and down appreciatively. "This one's gorgeous."

Izzy joined her, and took in the mare's long straight legs and gentle sloping shoulders.

"You have a good eye, you two," Courtney said, with a grin. "That's Seattle Surprise – our best racehorse. She's already won a couple of races for us this season."

"Oh, your mum had to come and check her out earlier," said Kate. "She was limping."

"No way!" Courtney groaned. "And with her big race coming up..."

"She's prepping for the Gresham Maiden Stakes at Clevedon Park Racetrack in a couple of weeks," Megan explained. "It's a pretty big race for us – the purse is $500,000."

"Purse?" Izzy looked confused.

"The prize money," said Courtney. "The 'purse' is what we call it out here."

"That's serious money," said Izzy.

"So who owns your horses?" Kate asked.

"We own some ourselves – Seattle Surprise, for instance – but the rest are owned by different people," Courtney replied. "We train more horses than we own. That's how we make our money."

"It's no wonder you need a security guard with such valuable horses around," Izzy joined in.

"Security guard? Where did you see him? What did he say to you?" Courtney spoke sharply.

"L-last night," Izzy stammered. "And he didn't say much, actually – just scared us half to death. He didn't seem to know who we were."

Courtney relaxed. "Sorry, I didn't mean to flip out – it's just that he's supposed to be kind of a secret. I guess Mom must have forgotten to tell him you were coming."

"Oh, I see." Izzy nodded, but she didn't see at all. A secret security guard?

"Lots of racing stables have security guards out here," said Megan, sensing the awkwardness in the air. "You're right, horses are valuable investments. Anyway, shall we get going?"

"Great!" Izzy exclaimed, glad to move on. But both she and Kate felt uneasy as they followed the twins out of the yard, for the next part of their tour.

Chapter 5

The Hard Work Begins

Kate and Izzy were kept busy all that first day in the yard. If they weren't organizing feeds or grooming horses, they were changing water buckets or cleaning tack. It was only when Sally said it was suppertime that they realized how tired they were.

"So how was your first day?" Sally asked, as they sat down to eat.

"Exhausting," Kate answered.

"I know what you mean." Sally looked worn out, too. "But you've made a good start. Thanks for all your help today. We'll have to organize a real schedule for tomorrow. It'd be a good idea if we could each take charge of a couple of horses – for mucking out and grooming at least."

"That's cool," said Courtney. "So long as I'm not in charge of Fiery Lad."

"Maybe I should look after him," Sally said. "He's not the easiest of horses."

"I don't mind looking after him." Izzy jumped in.

"Izzy, that's good of you," said Sally. "But are you sure you could manage him? He's sort of a handful."

Izzy bristled. "I know, but I'd love to give it a go."

"Hmm, maybe he'll behave for you," Sally said, pausing. "But if you hit problems, I'll take over."

Izzy had already decided there was no way she was going to let Sally take over.

"You could look after Frosty as well," Sally went on, "and Kate could take Sugarfoot and Tobago Bay."

"Great," Kate answered.

"That leaves me with Seattle, Ted with Lark's Song… Oh I'll figure out the rest later. We're all beat – why don't you go on up to bed?" Sally turned to

Courtney and Megan. "You two as well."

"What a day!" Izzy said, once they were safely in their room.

"I know," Kate agreed. "And with that stuff about schedules, it looks as if it's going to get even busier."

"I suppose it's all part of being at a racing stables."

"Guess so," said Kate. "But don't you think it's a bit weird that there isn't more stable help around?"

"Maybe they don't work at the weekend over here," said Izzy. She snuggled under her duvet and was drifting off when she remembered something. "Oh no! I've left Seattle Surprise's saddle out on the gate. Kate... Kate, can you hear me?"

But there was no answer – Kate had started running a bath. Izzy felt sleep washing over her again. Surely the saddle could wait until morning...

The next thing Izzy knew, Kate was shaking her. "Time to get up!"

"Ugh, what time *is* it?" Izzy groaned.

"Six-thirty," said Kate. "See you at breakfast!"

"I'm coming," said Izzy, hauling herself out of bed. Within five minutes, she was joining the others.

"Just in time," said Megan, passing her the toast.

The girls hurried through breakfast and set off to the stables.

"Mom will already be out on the training oval," Megan said, "so we'll get started with the jobs. Then how about watching the last half hour of training?"

"And perhaps even have a ride?" Izzy murmured.

"That sounds great, Megan," said Kate, glaring at her friend.

"Let's go," said Courtney.

"So, where's Ted this morning?" Izzy asked.

"Oh, he's probably in the office – he'll be out in a minute," Megan answered, striding ahead.

"Kate! Why did you glare at me?" Izzy demanded, once the twins were out of earshot.

"It's rude to ask for a ride," said Kate. "We are the guests here."

"All right, all right," Izzy grumbled, as they walked into the barn.

Izzy went to the first stall and led the big, bay mare into the aisle. Then she went back for Fiery Lad. While the horses were eating their breakfast, the girls started mucking out their stalls.

"Phew, it's hot in here," Izzy said as she finally finished, wiping the sweat off her forehead.

Kate grinned. "Let's go and find the twins."

"All done?" Courtney called across the yard.

"Yup," said Kate. "Now to see some racehorses."

It wasn't far to walk through the paddocks to the training oval behind the stables. Sally was in the middle, her eyes fixed on a string of six racehorses. The exercise riders crouched low in the saddles as they galloped around the outside of the track.

"The horses aren't going at full speed," Courtney explained. "They're just working out."

"It looks pretty fast to me," said Kate.

They waited for the horses to gallop past, and then Courtney led them into the middle of the oval.

"Check out Seattle!" Courtney pointed out the grey mare at the head of the string.

"How could we miss her!" Kate said.

The grey horse looked magnificent. Her sleek, muscular hindquarters pushed her onwards so fast that her delicate legs were little more than a blur.

"She looks great," breathed Izzy, watching in awe as Seattle Surprise's exercise rider fed her the reins and they swung around the turn.

"She sure does," Courtney said.

"Do you think we could go and watch her race?" Izzy asked excitedly.

"I don't see why not..." answered Courtney. "The racetrack's only fifty miles away from here."

"Brilliant!" Izzy exclaimed. But her good mood vanished when she saw Ted, the stable manager, ahead of them, holding a saddle and looking furious.

"I don't suppose you girls know anything about this?" he said, angrily. "It was left out last night."

Izzy's heart was pounding, but she said nothing.

"Maybe one of the exercise riders left it out yesterday morning," Megan suggested.

"But you girls were cleaning tack after that."

"Well, none of us left it out," said Courtney. "You know we'd tell you if we had, Ted."

Izzy swallowed hard. She wished she could just walk away, but she knew she had to own up. "Um, I think it might be my fault," she said. "I left it on the gate... I meant to go back for it but—"

"You just left it on the gate?" Ted thundered. "How could you have been so irresponsible? Don't you know how much these saddles cost?"

"It's all right, Ted," Sally called out, walking towards them. "I'll deal with this."

Sally put her arm around Izzy's shoulder as Ted stomped off with the saddle. "Look, we do have strict rules about putting tack back where it came from, but you weren't to know that."

Izzy nodded. She was almost crying. "I didn't do it on purpose," she said.

"I'm sure you didn't," Sally said. "And Ted didn't mean what he said. It's just that he's under so much pressure at the moment... Well, we all are... Come on, let's put it behind us and go enjoy ourselves."

Chapter 6

A Surprising Visitor

Izzy tried to follow Sally's advice that afternoon, but every time she saw Ted, she felt guilty and upset. The twins weren't as friendly as they had been, either, which made her feel worse. *It's because we're all working too hard to chat much*, she told herself. It was only when things were the same the next day and the one after, that Kate and Izzy started to feel more like hired hands than guests at Graytops.

On Wednesday morning, Kate poked her head over the stable door as Izzy was struggling to groom Fiery Lad, who was kicking and snorting in his stall.

"Need any help?"

"I'm fine," Izzy said, from somewhere behind the horse. "But I'd give anything for a ride..."

"Me too." Kate looked at her friend miserably. "It's work, work, work here, isn't it? And I can't understand why you were so determined to look after that horse, Izzy. Why don't you just give in?"

"No way," Izzy said firmly. "I can handle him."

"But clearly you *can't*," Kate said. "You've been in here for an hour, trying to pick his feet out."

"I'll be all right," Izzy flared up. "If only they'd get more help around here, things would be better. We need someone we can ask advice, but Ted's so unfriendly. And where are all the stable hands?"

"Not a clue," Kate said thoughtfully. "I was wondering that too, but it seems rude to ask. Everyone else is working just as hard as we are."

"I know, but this is the twins' farm, and Ted's getting paid for it! Will you keep *still*, Fiery Lad?" Izzy cried, giving the horse's lead-rope a sharp tug.

The whites of Fiery Lad's eyes flashed and he

reared up on his hind legs. Izzy, totally unprepared, turned as white as a sheet as the horse reared again and again, whinnying loudly. What if Ted heard?

"Get out of there, Izzy," Kate pleaded.

"Hush, sssshh boy," crooned Izzy, quickly joining Kate as the horse thrashed around in the stall.

"We should get help," said Kate.

"No, wait a moment," Izzy cried. "He'll be all right in a second."

But Fiery Lad's frenzy wasn't easing off, and Izzy was just starting to panic when she heard footsteps at the end of the barn. She turned to see a girl standing there, and watched, frozen, as the girl rushed down the aisle, drew back the bolt on Fiery Lad's stall and dashed inside.

Izzy and Kate watched, amazed, as she calmed the frantic horse. Finally, the girl stood, cradling Fiery Lad's snuffling nose in her hand.

"Take it easy, dude," she murmured gently. "You're all right now."

"That was incredible!" Izzy said.

"Tricks of the trade." The girl smiled.

Izzy and Kate looked at the girl, who could only be a few years older than they were. She'd handled that horse like a professional.

"Paula! Where did you go?" a voice rang out.

"Fiery Lad should be all right now. I'll catch you two later," she said, and walked off.

Izzy glanced at Kate. "She was nice. Wonder who she was?"

"No idea," Kate said. "But she calmed him down."

"She did, didn't she?" Izzy lifted up Fiery Lad's foot gently and scraped a stone out of his shoe. "She's the first visitor we've seen since we got here."

They heard footsteps at the end of the barn and turned to see three people coming towards them.

"It's Sally. I'm going to be in such trouble if that girl's told her..." Izzy said.

"Hi Izzy... Kate," Sally said, smiling. "Let me introduce you to our vet, Dr. Doyle, and his assistant, Paula." She pointed to the man and the girl they'd just met. "This is Kate and Izzy – they've come all the way from England on a visit."

"Hi there," the vet said. "He can be quite a handful, can't he?" He gestured to Fiery Lad.

"Izzy's doing an amazing job with him," said Sally.

Izzy breathed a sigh of relief. Paula clearly hadn't told her what had happened.

"Come on, Eric." Sally turned back to the vet. "Let's go and take a look at the yearlings."

Paula stayed behind, stroking Fiery Lad.

"Thanks a million for not saying anything to Sally," Izzy said.

"There wasn't anything to say." The girl grinned.

"You were brilliant with him," Izzy said. "Where did you learn to manage horses like that?"

"From my dad, I guess. He's been working with racehorses all his life. It must be in my genes." Paula laughed. "Hey, I'll give you a hand." She picked up a broom. "So when did you two get here?"

"Saturday," Izzy answered. "We're quite new to the world of racehorses."

"I'm new at Graytops as well," Paula said. "I've

only been working for Dr. Doyle for a few months. My home's back in New York State."

"Oh right." Izzy nodded. Paula looked confident, but she sounded as unsure of herself as they were. "So is this a summer job?"

"I wanted to go to veterinary college, but my folks couldn't afford the fees," she said sadly. "This is the next best thing. Dr. Doyle's been good to me."

"Are you guys finished in there?" Courtney called, and then she noticed Paula and her smile vanished. "Oh, you're here."

Izzy looked up, surprised. Was she mistaken or was there a change in Courtney's voice when she spoke to Paula? It was unfriendly... icy even.

"Hi, Courtney," Paula said. "Dr. Doyle's with your mom, so I just thought I'd take the time to meet your new friends. How's it going?"

"Oh you know, not too bad."

Izzy could almost feel the tension in the air. She was relieved when she heard Megan's voice coming from the other end of the barn.

"Oh no, has Dr. Doyle left? Don't tell me I've missed him. I wanted to ask him something."

"He's with Mom in the paddocks. Let's find him. You coming?" Courtney turned to Izzy and Kate.

"We'll just finish up here and then we'll be right with you," Izzy answered, as the twins hurried off.

"They're an... interesting pair..." said Paula.

"That's one way of putting it," Izzy said. "Do I get the impression you don't like them much?"

"I think it's more a case of them not liking me," Paula said. "They've been a little weird with me, well, ever since the incident with Seattle really."

"What incident?" Izzy was puzzled.

"One afternoon, I thought Seattle was colicking, so I called Sally over. Seems it was just in time."

Izzy was full of admiration. Her own horse had nearly died of colic because she hadn't been quick enough to spot the symptoms.

"Courtney and Megan sure didn't like the praise I got for it. You'd have thought they'd be happy that I'd saved their horse, but I think they thought

I was butting in. They've been real cool ever since."

"How silly," Izzy said. "It doesn't matter who saved the horse as long as it was saved."

"That's what I thought," Paula went on. "But, hey, I'm sure the twins are really nice, underneath it all." She paused. "Would you two like to go to the movies sometime? I could do with some friends here."

Izzy didn't answer. She and Kate were guests of Megan and Courtney. It wouldn't look good if they made friends with someone the twins didn't like.

"Should I take it that's a 'yes' then?" Paula winked.

"Definitely," Kate said, nudging her friend. "You were so kind to cover for Izzy like that."

"Great! Well, I guess I'd better find Dr. Doyle. See you later." And, with that, she was gone.

"So you really think we should go?" Izzy asked.

"I don't see why not," said Kate. "She seems friendly, and it's not our quarrel."

"I suppose..." Izzy said. If Courtney and Megan were meant to be their friends, they were making a lot less effort than Paula.

Chapter 7

An Old Friend

"I'm shattered." Kate leaned on her broom.

"Me too," Izzy replied. "And it's so hot!"

They had just spent their fifth day of running around, wheeling barrows of straw, filling water buckets, sweeping up...

"Do you think we'll get to go out for a ride this afternoon?" Izzy said.

Kate shrugged. "They haven't asked us yet."

"It's so annoying," Izzy said, crossly. "Anyone would think we were being paid to work here!"

"Do you think we got the wrong end of the stick

about it being a holiday?" Kate said.

"It was a prize, and you wouldn't expect a prize to be just work, would you? And remember all the riding that Megan and Courtney talked about in their letters? Something doesn't add up here," Izzy mused. "I think we should say something."

The twins joined them a few minutes later.

"Hi guys," Courtney said with a broad smile. "It's been a tough day, today."

"You can say that again," said Kate, half-scowling.

"Look," Megan started. "We're sorry you haven't had a chance to go out for a ride yet. We thought we might go for a long trail ride tomorrow. We could take a picnic lunch and ride up into the hills."

"That sounds great!" Izzy and Kate chorused together. "Can't wait."

The next day, Izzy drew back the curtains with a totally different feeling.

"Kate," she cried. "We're riding this morning."

"At last!" Kate replied.

The two girls dressed and hurried downstairs. Again, the kitchen was empty.

"I suppose Courtney and Megan must have gone across to the stables ahead of us to get ready," Izzy said. "Do you think they're getting Prince and Garnet tacked up?"

"Fat chance!" said Kate, quickly making two hot chocolates.

Izzy barely touched hers. "Come on, let's go."

In their haste, they didn't notice that Sally's car wasn't in its usual spot, but as they turned the corner to the stables, they did notice that it was very quiet.

"Where are they?" said Izzy. "Courtney! Megan! We're here."

"Oh, it's you," Ted called. "I wondered when you two might make it out to do some work."

"Are we late for something specific?" Izzy asked. The man's rudeness was getting to her.

"Well, you're not exactly late but the horses do need to be taken out to the paddocks."

"But where are Courtney and Megan?" Kate

asked. "We're meant to be riding with them."

"The girls have had to go out with Sally. They'll be back by three."

"Three!" Kate gasped. "What do we do till then?"

"As I said – those horses need to be taken out, and then there's the stalls to clean and all of the water buckets to be filled. That should keep you both busy." With that, Ted was gone.

Izzy was fuming. "They haven't even texted us to let us know, and they've left us with all the work! Well, they can forget it!"

"Come on, Izzy," Kate said. "Ted's obviously under a lot of pressure and the work's got to be done."

"He can do it himself," Izzy said, standing with her hands on her hips.

"The horses will be the ones to suffer," Kate reminded her.

"I don't care." Izzy frowned. But she did care, very much. "I know you're right – we *have* to help. It's just that everything's so awful out here."

"I know," Kate said, sadly. "I can't help thinking

about all the riding we'd be doing if we were home."

"Yes, I've thought that too." Izzy rubbed her eyes. She felt like crying. "Hey, I've got an idea that might cheer us up. What time is it now?"

"Eight o'clock," Kate said, looking puzzled.

"That's two o'clock at home," said Izzy. "Everyone will be at Sandy Lane. Let's ring them – give them a surprise. We can find out how they did at Colcott!"

"I don't know." Kate was hesitant. "It's really expensive to call from a mobile, isn't it?"

"It'll be worth it, to cheer ourselves up," Izzy said. "Mum said I should call if I really needed to. Then we'll start mucking out."

"Call *her* perhaps, not Sandy Lane," said Kate. "Oh go on then."

"Here goes," Izzy said, punching in the number.

"Hello, Sandy Lane Stables..."

"Is that Rosie?" Izzy said excitedly. "It's me, Izzy! How's it going over there?"

"Hi, Izzy. Everything's great and—"

"What about Midnight?" Izzy broke in.

"He's fine," Rosie replied. "Missing you."

"And how did you all do at Colcott?"

"Jess came second in the Tack-and-Turnout, and Alex came third in the Working Hunter, and the new girl – Clare Testar – won the Under 13.2 Hands. Oh and then Midnight and I—"

"Yes?" Izzy said impatiently.

"We won the Open Jumping!" Rosie sounded pleased but a little embarrassed.

"You won? Brilliant!" Izzy cried. It was great that Rosie had won, but she couldn't help thinking that if she'd been home, it would have been her.

"So how's it all going?" Rosie asked. "Are you riding real racehorses? Is it really hot?"

"Yeah, it's baking," Izzy said, tentatively. "But, well, Graytops is a bit different from a riding stables."

"I bet you're having an amazing time though."

"Oh, yes of course we are," said Izzy. Suddenly, the phone call seemed a bad idea. She could hardly tell Rosie how miserable they both were. Everyone would be upset, and Sarah would feel awful about it.

"So I don't expect you'll want to come home then?" Rosie asked jokingly.

"Definitely not." Izzy laughed nervously.

"Look, I don't mean to be rude," Rosie added, "but I'm going to have to go. The one o'clock hack's just come in and the yard's in absolute chaos."

"Of course," Izzy said with relief. "We've got to go ourselves, actually."

"Another racehorse waiting?" Rosie giggled.

"Hmm, something like that," Izzy said. "Okay, bye... See you in a couple of weeks."

She hung up, and looked at Kate. "Everyone expects us to be having such a wonderful time out here, and it's not our fault that we're not. I think we should have a talk with Courtney and Megan when they get back. There's nothing to stop us from changing our flights and going home early, is there?"

"No, but perhaps we should give Courtney and Megan a chance to explain first," Kate said.

"Okay. There's something very strange going on here – and I want to know what it is."

At five o'clock, Izzy and Kate finally heard the sound of wheels on gravel. Sally and the twins were back.

"Oh, there you are," Courtney said, breathlessly, racing into the sitting room. "Ready for a ride?"

"We *were* ready." Izzy sat, stony-faced. "Hours and hours ago."

"Yes, look, we're really sorry, but something super important came up," Courtney apologized. "Still, we can go out now, can't we?"

"It's a bit late, isn't it?" said Izzy.

"Don't be silly," Megan said. "The sun will be up for a few more hours still."

"Unless you don't want to?" Courtney added.

"We've been wanting to ride all week, you know that!" Izzy exploded. "You've treated us like hired hands, and we're not even getting paid! We're doing all the work that stable hands normally do, and more. We wish we'd never come and we've decided to change our flights and go home early." She folded her arms defiantly.

"Oh no, don't do that," Courtney said, hastily.

"I know it hasn't been the greatest here. Dad wanted to cancel your trip, but Mom said we couldn't."

"Your dad did?" Izzy was intrigued. This was the first time the twins had mentioned their father.

"Yes – our Dad. We have got one, you know," Courtney snapped.

"So why *didn't* he cancel it, if your parents are having, well, personal problems?" asked Kate.

"Personal problems? They don't have personal problems!" Courtney sounded horrified.

"Where *is* your father then?" Izzy blurted out.

"Uh... he had to move out," Courtney said vaguely. "But it's not because of Mom."

"If you'd tell us what's going on, we might be able to understand," Kate said, feeling frustrated.

"But Mom and Dad don't want us to talk about it," said Megan, looking worriedly at her sister.

"Things have changed, Megan," said Courtney, gently. "We owe it to Izzy and Kate to tell them."

"Okay," said Megan, after a moment. "I guess we'd better sit down and talk."

Chapter 8

A Revelation and a Decision

Courtney took a deep breath. "We'll have to go back a few months..."

"Things were going really well at the farm," Megan began. "We were on a real winning streak. It had taken a while for Dad to build up a reputation, but more and more people were sending their horses to him here..."

"And then Sugarfoot tested positive for an antihistamine drug after a big race," Courtney said.

Izzy gasped. "At home, a horse isn't allowed to

race with any kind of drug in its system. It might act as a stimulant and give the horse an unfair advantage."

"Same here," Courtney said, "except for anti-inflammatory drugs, you know, sort of painkillers."

"So what happened next?" Kate asked.

"Well," Megan said, "Dad was called before the track stewards and asked to explain, but Sugarfoot hadn't been on any sort of prescription so he had no idea how the antihistamine could have gotten into her system. Dad didn't have a previous record, and the drug was only a class five—"

"The lowest type of drug offence," put in Courtney.

Megan nodded. "So the stewards decided they wouldn't suspend him. They only fined him, but Sugarfoot was still disqualified and placed last – and the owner lost the whole purse."

"Dad was lucky it was only a class five drug," said Courtney. "A class one drug carries a $5,000 fine and up to five years' suspension for the trainer."

Izzy was shocked. "So how *did* the antihistamine get into her system then?"

"That's what we keep asking ourselves," Megan said, looking sadly at her twin.

"The only thing Dad could do was to get rid of all the casual staff," Courtney went on.

"So *that's* why you have so little stable help here," Izzy said, as everything fell into place.

"Yeah, there were a lot of really unhappy people without jobs, but Dad had no choice," said Megan. "As it turned out, it was all for nothing as it happened again a month later – this time with Tobago Bay."

Kate and Izzy looked appalled.

"But this time it was way worse," Megan said. "This time it was the class three drug benzocaine."

"MEGAN!" Courtney hissed. "Dad didn't want us telling *anyone* that outside the family." She paused. "Anyway, he got a $1,500 fine and a three month suspension – which is why he's not at the farm."

Izzy let out a low whistle. "That's awful."

"Mom's taken over as temporary trainer," Megan explained. "It's been really hard for her..."

"But this is so unfair," Kate said. "If your father

knows nothing about the drugs, why should he have to leave his home?"

"You've got to think how it looks to the stewards," Courtney replied. "A trainer is responsible for the condition of his horses, which includes making sure no one has a chance to give them an illegal drug."

"So that's why you've got the security guard? To protect the horses?" Izzy said.

"Yup." Courtney nodded. "A lot of farms have security guards, but we've never needed one before. I'm sorry I acted so weird when you mentioned him – it's just that Mom wants him to stay out of sight. If anyone unusual turns up at the yard, she wants to be able to catch them."

"Yes, of course," said Izzy.

"We just can't risk it happening again," Megan joined in. "We've already had owners take their horses away. In fact, that was why we couldn't come to meet you at the airport."

"The trailer!" Izzy exclaimed, remembering the horse they'd seen being loaded on their first night.

"You'd have thought that our owners would have given Dad the benefit of the doubt," Megan said angrily. "But drugs are a dirty word. And now, people have even started saying that all the other Graytops' horses must have won while they were on drugs too – designer drugs that couldn't be detected in the usual tests."

"But that's crazy," Kate cried.

"Of course it's crazy," Megan agreed. "But think how it looks. And what if it happens again? Seattle Surprise runs in her big race next week. It would be the end for Graytops if she tested positive. We'd lose even more owners. We'd have to sell the farm. It's too awful to consider." She was almost crying now.

"All right, Megan," Courtney said, laying a hand on her sister's shoulder. "It's not going to come to that. Seattle will be fine when she runs."

"But what if she isn't?" Megan sobbed. "What happens then?"

"We just can't think like that," Courtney said firmly. She turned to Kate and Izzy. "Look, I'm really sorry we weren't here for your ride this morning. We had to go with Mom to see the stewards at Clevedon Park to smooth things over. She didn't want to go by herself."

"Yes, I understand," Izzy murmured. "What did the stewards say?"

"Well, they're letting us run Seattle next week," Courtney said. "So that's something."

"This is a lot for you two to take in." Megan pulled herself together. "If it's going to be too much for you, I'm sure you'll be able to change your tickets."

"But we'd love you to stay," Courtney joined in. "We don't know how we'd have managed without all your help, actually. And of course we'd try and make sure you got to do plenty of riding..."

"Why don't you and Kate take Prince and Garnet out now?" Megan suggested. "You could talk it over and make a decision."

"Good idea," Izzy said, though the second Megan had suggested it might be 'too much' for them, Izzy had determined to stay.

"This feels good," Izzy said a while later, twisting round in the saddle to call back to Kate. "I'd almost forgotten what it felt like to sit on a horse!"

"Me too." Kate laughed as she clucked Prince on down the grassy lanes between the paddocks. The sun was low in the sky, casting the farm in a soft golden light. "So, what do you think?" she said, pushing Prince into a trot through a line of lime trees.

"I don't really know," Izzy replied. "I mean... I never imagined anything like this could be going on. No wonder everyone's so stressed."

"But what if the Bryants really have been doping their horses?" Kate asked, nervously. "I hate to say it, but we don't want to stay with dishonest trainers."

Izzy bent to pat Garnet's neck. "I don't think they are dishonest. Besides, it doesn't make any sense. They know all horses get tested at the end of a race."

"And surely Sarah wouldn't be friends with people who were capable of something like doping?"

Izzy looked thoughtful. "I don't think she would. And do you remember when Rosie got caught up in that doping scandal at home?"

A couple of years earlier, Rosie had made friends with a local stable lad who was on the run, accused of trying to dope a racehorse. It turned out that a rival trainer was responsible.

"Of course I do," said Kate, nodding. "A rival trainer could be involved here too."

"I wonder who trained the horses that came in second in each race, for instance." Izzy frowned. "We must ask Courtney and Megan."

"So it's a 'no' to going home early?" Kate said.

"Definitely. You heard what Courtney said – we'll get to ride a lot more now, and we might even help them get to the bottom of things."

"Oh Izzy." Kate groaned as she gathered up Prince's reins. "I'm not sure we should get more involved in this. Anyway, we've done enough talking for one day. Let's gallop!"

They clattered back into the yard in high spirits.

"Come on," Izzy said, jumping down from

Garnet's saddle and leading the little pony off. "Let's get these ponies rubbed down and find Courtney and Megan."

When the girls eventually headed back to the house, it was already dusk.

"Courtney... Megan," Kate called, in the hallway.

"Up here," a voice called down. Izzy and Kate climbed the stairs to Courtney's bedroom.

"Is your mum around?" Kate whispered.

"Mom's on the phone to Dad in the study," Courtney said. "It's fine to talk. She knows you know the whole story."

"And did she mind?" said Izzy.

"She was kinda worried about you being dragged into it all," Megan said. "But then she realized we couldn't keep it a secret any longer."

"So, are you going or staying?" asked Courtney.

"Staying," Kate answered. "We want to help."

"Awesome!" Courtney's face lit up.

"And we have a hunch," Izzy said. "You see, we've come across something like this before."

"There was a racehorse at the local racing stables who was being doped," added Kate. "It caused a massive stir at Sandy Lane."

"Our friend Rosie met this stable boy who was accused of having doped a horse," Izzy explained. "It turned out it wasn't him at all, but a rival trainer."

"And you think the same thing might be happening here?" Courtney said.

"Well yes," Izzy said. "What about the trainer of the horses that came in second?"

"The trainer – Joe Hagan – is a friend of our family's. He wouldn't do anything to hurt Dad."

"But do you know that?" Izzy said. "What if he has money troubles, or holds some kind of grudge?"

"It just isn't possible," said Courtney, bluntly.

"Joe isn't like that," Megan added. "He isn't, and Seattle will be just fine in the race, so let's forget it."

And that, it seemed, was that. Both the twins had sounded so certain... If Izzy and Kate hadn't seen the worried look in their eyes, they might almost have believed them.

Chapter 9

An Unusual Offer

"Courtney and Megan didn't want to listen to our hunch about who it could be," Izzy moaned the following day.

"Joe Hagan is a friend of their father's," said Kate. "Think how we'd feel if they accused one of our Sandy Lane friends of something this bad."

"I suppose so," Izzy said. "But I still can't believe how narrow-minded they're being."

"We should try to understand how upset they are over all this. If they're sure Joe isn't involved, we should drop it."

"But I can't bear just sitting around doing nothing," Izzy replied.

"It doesn't look like you're sitting doing nothing to me," a voice called from the other end of the barn.

Izzy and Kate both turned. "Paula!" They smiled, pleased to see the vet's assistant. It was good to see a friendly face. "What are you doing here?"

"Oh, Dr. Doyle's come to check on Seattle Surprise, so I thought I'd come and see you. Are you by yourselves?"

Kate nodded. "Courtney and Megan have gone out for a ride."

"And left you to do all of the hard work?"

"We've done loads of riding this weekend," said Kate quickly. "And Courtney and Megan really needed a break."

"Of course." Paula winked. "Only joking."

At that moment, Ted appeared at the end of the barn. "I thought I could hear another voice."

"Only me," Paula began, but before she could say another word, Ted had marched off. "Hmm, not the friendliest guy in the world, is he?" she said.

"You can say that again," Izzy muttered.

"Don't let him get you down. What were you two chatting about when I came in?" asked Paula. "It sounded important."

Izzy hesitated. "We've just found out some stuff about Graytops, that's all."

"Oh, you mean all the stuff about the doping? It's terrible, isn't it? Their whole business is at stake."

Izzy looked at Kate. Should they tell Paula their theory about it being a rival trainer? She seemed sensible. Kate looked back at Izzy and nodded.

"Well, we had an idea," Izzy started. "We came across something like this back home – at our local racing stables."

"A horse was being doped," said Kate. "It turned out to be a rival trainer and we thought... well, what if it was the same here?"

Paula looked thoughtful, but didn't say anything.

"Courtney and Megan were really cross when we suggested it," Kate went on. "You see the trainer of both of the horses that came in second each time was a man named Joe Hagan. Quite a coincidence, but Courtney and Megan are convinced he can't be involved. They insist he's a friend of their dad's."

"I know Joe Hagan," said Paula, scratching her head. "His stable's not that far from here. I've been there with Dr. Doyle. You know, I don't like him. He's a real piece of work if you ask me. And if the Bryants had to close down their farm he'd probably get some of their horses. No, I wouldn't trust him as far as I could throw him."

"Really?" Izzy cast a quick glance at Kate. This was getting interesting.

"Really," Paula confirmed. "He's always arguing over our bills... Says we're overcharging him. I don't know why Dr. Doyle keeps going back there."

"So perhaps Joe Hagan is struggling financially?" Izzy said.

"Well, I don't know about that," Paula said quickly. "But I don't think he's as squeaky clean as Courtney and Megan seem to think. If you want to help them, why don't you go and check out Joe Hagan's farm yourselves? You never know what you might find..."

"We couldn't go behind Courtney and Megan's backs," Izzy said quickly. "Besides, we wouldn't know how to get there."

"I'll drive you," Paula said.

"We couldn't exactly turn up at Joe Hagan's farm uninvited, could we?" said Kate. "What would we say? Excuse me, are you doping the Bryants' horses?"

"Of course not!" Paula laughed. "But Joe Hagan doesn't lock up the stable yard, and there isn't a security guard. We could go there at night."

"We?" Kate asked.

"I'd come with you."

"Paula, it's really nice of you to offer to help, but I don't think we can do that," said Kate. She looked at Izzy, waiting for her to agree: she didn't.

"Oh, okay. I understand. I'll go on my own." Paula looked hurt. "I'd better get out to the paddocks. Dr. Doyle will be wondering where I am." She paused. "Hey – do you guys wanna go to the movies with me, maybe sometime this week?"

"That sounds brilliant," said Izzy, upset to see their new friend so low.

"How about Wednesday?"

"Wednesday sounds good." Izzy nodded.

"I'll come pick you up at around seven-thirty," Paula said. "See you then."

As soon as she had left, Kate turned to Izzy. "You do think we did the right thing, don't you?" she said. "Turning down Paula's suggestion to go over to Joe Hagan's place?"

"Well, I suppose it would be terrible if we were caught. But... what if we weren't?"

Kate's heart sank. If anyone was up for that sort of challenge, it was Izzy.

Chapter 10

Stakeout

Sally was so preoccupied with Seattle's training that it wasn't until Wednesday afternoon that Kate and Izzy had a chance to talk to her about their plans to go to the cinema with Paula.

"Sure you can," said Sally. "It'll be good for you to have a break, but you must be back by ten."

"So where are you two going?" Megan slid into the kitchen in her socks, nibbling a carrot.

"To see a film," said Kate. "With Paula."

Courtney scowled. "Huh, good luck with that."

"Just what is it that you and Megan don't like

about Paula?" asked Izzy.

"Oh, it's nothing important."

"No, come on." Izzy pushed, annoyed. "I mean, she's been nothing but nice to us since we arrived, and it's hard for her, being new around here."

Courtney grimaced. "Maybe you don't know her as well as we do."

"I'd have thought you'd be grateful that she saved Seattle's life," Izzy blurted out.

"Izzy!" said Kate, fearing that her friend might have overstepped the mark.

"What exactly do you mean *saved Seattle's life?*" demanded Courtney.

"Just what I said."

"Ha... Is that what she told you?" Courtney chuckled to herself.

"Yes, it is." Izzy looked at her defiantly.

"Then she's a better liar than I thought she was."

"Don't get into this, Courtney," Megan begged.

"But why would she lie about it?" Izzy wanted to know. "She told us that she recognized the symptoms of colic, she called your mum, and you two didn't like the praise she got for it."

Courtney snorted. "Paula wouldn't know the symptoms of colic if they hit her in the face. I was the one who told Mom."

"It's true." Megan supported her sister. "Courtney saved Seattle's life."

"Leave it, Izzy." Kate stepped in, seeing a quarrel about to erupt. "We ought to get ready."

Izzy followed Kate to the door sheepishly. Who was telling the truth? They had been getting on better with the twins, too. Had she just blown it?

"Well, you know how to put someone's back up, don't you?" said Kate, once they were upstairs.

"She had it coming to her," Izzy muttered, feeling a little guilty. "All those sneaky comments."

"I wonder why they do hate Paula so much?"

"I don't know," Izzy said. "You saw how brilliant she was with Fiery Lad."

"I did. It all seems so weird, but—"

A car horn beeped. It was Paula, in an old Cadillac.

Izzy rushed to the window. "She's here already and I haven't even brushed my hair! Oh, cool car."

The girls bolted down the stairs, shouting out their goodbyes.

"Don't forget – be home by ten," called Sally.

"What a great movie," Paula said, as they came out of the cinema. "Izzy, are you okay? You're really quiet tonight."

Izzy hesitated. She had to say something. "Paula, you remember you told us about when you saved Seattle's life? Well..." Izzy started slowly. "I had a bit of an argument with Courtney this evening. She said she was the one who'd saved Seattle, not you."

"Well she would, wouldn't she? She hates me! They both do!" Paula exclaimed, clearly upset. "Do you believe her?"

"Of course we don't," Izzy said, and she meant it, seeing Paula's face. Nobody could act that well.

"Good," Paula said, sniffing. "Let's change the subject, then. I was thinking I might go over to Joe

Hagan's farm after I drop you off. I'm sure it will be fine, but... this sounds silly, but I just wish I had a friend who could sit in the car outside and keep watch for me."

Izzy hesitated. "I suppose we could. We did tell you the whole rival trainer idea, and if we stay outside, we're not trespassing."

"We've got to be back by ten," Kate pointed out.

"Easy," said Paula. "Joe's farm is on the way back."

A few minutes later, Izzy and Kate were being driven down a winding road. Finally, the car ground to a halt alongside a wall. Paula turned to face them. "Wish me luck."

"I'm coming with you," Izzy said, suddenly.

"Are you sure?" asked Paula.

"Positive," Izzy said. "You stay with the car, Kate."

"But Izzy..." Kate called plaintively. It was too late. She watched them spring onto the wall and sank back in her seat. This was such a bad idea...

"Don't worry, I'm sure we won't get caught," Paula

told Izzy, sounding convinced.

"Do they have guard dogs?" Izzy asked, feeling a little less brave as they clambered over the wall.

"Nothing like that. Now, the stable yard is to the left of us." Paula flicked on a flashlight to light their way across to the farm buildings.

Unsteadily, Izzy crunched across the gravel, regretting her impulsive offer to join Paula.

"This is the plan," Paula whispered. "We look in the office together, then I'll look around the yard as I know my way about. We can meet back in the car in ten minutes."

Izzy nodded. "Okay, let's go."

They crept across the yard, hearts thumping. Once they got into the office, Paula shone her flashlight around the room. "Hmm, where should we start?" she murmured, pulling open the top drawer of the desk.

Holding the flashlight in one hand, she began rummaging through the drawer with the other.

Izzy watched her, frozen with fear. "What are we

looking for?" she asked, her voice shaking slightly.

Paula shrugged. "Evidence of drugs? Anything..."

Izzy took a deep breath and made her way to a filing cabinet on the other side of the room, pulling out drawer after drawer. Papers upon papers looked out at her – veterinary receipts, training bills, breeding certificates...

"Nothing useful here," Paula said. "I'm going to the yard. I'll leave you with the flashlight."

Izzy looked up, and heard the click of the door shutting behind Paula. She crept over to the desk, her legs shaking, picked up the flashlight and sat down in the chair. The flashlight beam swung over a computer and some pens, and then it lit up a sticky note. Izzy leaned forward to read it and gasped. She was peeling the note from the desk when she heard footsteps crunching on gravel. Someone was coming! In a second she had switched off the flashlight and ducked under the desk.

"I heard voices in here," a man's voice boomed out as the light came on.

Izzy felt sick. It had to be Joe Hagan.

"You must have imagined it, Joe," a woman said.

"You can never be too careful," said the man.

Izzy peeped out from under the desk and drew her breath in sharply. She hadn't closed the top drawer of the filing cabinet. If they noticed that, they'd be sure to come right into the room. Now she held her breath in panic... One... two... three...

"There's nothing in here. I must be hearing things," the man said.

The light went off. Izzy didn't dare move. She had to get back to the car before anything else happened, but her legs felt like jelly. She'd almost been caught! And was Paula all right? What if Joe Hagan saw her?

Izzy pulled up the sleeve of her shirt. The numbers on her watch dial glowed, plain and clear: ten o'clock. She should have been back at the car by now.

Izzy crept out from under the desk, stood up and looked out of the office window. The yard was as dark as pitch. It was now or never. Slowly, ever so slowly, she turned the office door handle and ran...

Chapter 11

Trouble

Kate looked at her watch anxiously. It was ten o'clock and Paula and Izzy still weren't back. They were going to be seriously late getting back to Graytops and Sally was going to be furious.

"Come on," she muttered to herself, tapping her finger on the car window.

And then she saw a face on top of the wall – Paula's face. "Where's Izzy?" Kate hissed.

"Ssshh," Paula said. "They'll hear you."

"They? Who?" Kate said, panicking.

"Joe Hagan and his wife... They're out there."

"And you've left Izzy inside?" Kate was shocked.

"Ten more minutes and we'll go after her."

It felt the longest ten minutes of Kate's life. Finally, Izzy's face appeared over the wall, pinched and pale.

"Oh Izzy," Kate cried. "Thank goodness."

"That was close," Izzy said, tiptoeing to the car.

"Did you find something?" Kate asked.

"I did, and I think it could be important."

Kate frowned as Izzy handed her the sticky note.

"I found this on the desk," Izzy told her.

"It's Ted's name and mobile number." Kate gasped.

"And why would he have given Joe Hagan his mobile number?" asked Izzy. "They work at rival stables and Ted isn't the friendliest of people."

"It does seem weird," Paula said. "I don't think they know each other at all."

Izzy nodded. "Ted was the only person kept on after the doping, wasn't he?"

"That's because Sally trusts him," said Kate.

"I've never liked him," said Izzy. "He was so mean

about that saddle."

"He's not friendly, but that doesn't make him guilty," Kate said.

"No, but this might," Izzy said slowly. "All we have to do now is catch him."

"Whoa, hang on a minute," Paula said. "What do you mean, *catch him*? The best thing to do is to go to Sally with this."

"It's not enough proof. It's just a phone number," Kate said. "The Bryant family think the world of Ted, don't they, Izzy?"

"Yeah, for some strange reason, they do." Izzy nodded. "And I have to say I agree with everything you've said. Also, we can't tell Sally where we've been tonight – she'd go mad."

"But what about Seattle?" Paula said, looking worried. "We'll be leaving her totally at Ted's mercy if he's doing the doping."

"We'll watch Ted night and day until the race," Kate said. "We're going to need more proof before we can accuse him of anything."

They drove home in silence, but Izzy and Kate could sense Paula didn't like their plan.

They were half an hour late getting back to Graytops and realized they needed a good excuse. They certainly couldn't tell the truth.

"Maybe Sally will already be in bed," Izzy said. "She's always so tired."

"I think that's unlikely, with us to worry about," Kate replied. "And the lights are on. Here goes."

"Where on earth have you been?" Sally cried, as soon as she saw them. "The movie finished ages ago. We were worried you'd been in an accident."

"We're really sorry. We, er, lost track of time," Izzy said, rather feebly. "We went for a burger afterwards."

"I said be back by ten," Sally said firmly. "You could have texted me, at least. Just wait till I see Paula. It's time for bed, the pair of you."

Sally was no happier the next morning. "Okay, so you lost track of time." She looked tired as she ran her hand through her hair. "But you worried us."

Kate and Izzy sat at the table, shamefaced.

"I don't have any more time to discuss it," Sally went on as they murmured apologies once more. "I have more important things to think about – like Seattle's race on Tuesday. So, let's put it behind us and join Courtney and Megan at the barn. We—" She stopped as her mobile rang. "Hi Doug. Yes, sweetie, everything's fine..." Sally began, waving the girls away. Gratefully, they bolted for the yard.

"Courtney... Megan," Izzy called, when she saw the twins.

"What?" Courtney snapped. "Mom's in such a bad mood because of you."

Thud! Splash!

Garnet had kicked his water bucket across the ground with such a deafening clatter that they couldn't help laughing.

"Oh man!" Courtney said. "You silly old nag." She turned to Izzy and Kate. "Can you two start mucking out?" she asked, still smiling. "Then go and find Ted. He's already out on the oval I think."

"Oh, we'll find him," Izzy said, looking at Kate.

The two girls kept a close watch on Ted over the next few days, but were surprised to see that he seemed to be leaving Sally to look after Seattle Surprise. On Saturday morning, a real treat awaited them – the ride they'd been dreaming of. Sally said they could join the exercise string – riding Sugarfoot and Lark's Song. Izzy and Kate were full of excitement as they groomed the two horses with extra care.

"I'm just going to get Lark's Song's saddle," Izzy said, making her way across the yard and humming to herself. This was going to be such a great day.

As she went into the tack room, she thought she could hear a voice, but Kate was in the barn and everyone else had left for the training oval. She listened again: nothing.

"I must have been imagining it," she thought, disappearing into the tack room. She took down the saddle and hurried back outside. She was about to go into the barn, when she heard the voice again.

It was coming from the office and whoever was talking was speaking in low tones, as if he or she didn't want to be overheard.

Izzy crept across the yard until she was just a little way away from the office. She took a deep breath, looked in through the window and saw...

Ted! He had his back turned to her and he was talking very quietly into his mobile. His voice was muffled, but she could tell he was angry. Suddenly he turned to face the window. Izzy ducked.

"I'll fight you every step of the way... I can't get you that kind of money... But that would kill her!"

Izzy's heart began to thump and everything started swimming in front of her eyes. Ted was talking about killing Seattle! Just as she was sure she was going to pass out, the office door flew open.

"Who's that... Who's there?"

Izzy froze to the spot. Ted stood and stared at her.

"What do you think you're doing?" he shouted.

"Um, I came to get Lark's Song's saddle..."

"You were listening to my call, weren't you?"

"No, I wasn't, I mean... I didn't hear anything... I was coming to look for you. Kate was having problems tacking up Sugarfoot and..." Izzy felt herself getting hysterical.

"Calm down," Ted said, his voice softening. "It's not the end of the world." He gave her a strange, crooked smile which scared Izzy even more. "I'll come and give you a hand. Here, let me carry that."

He went to take the saddle, but Izzy shrank away. Puzzled, he led the way back to the barn. "I've scared you, haven't I?" he said.

"No, it's just... I..."

"Well I'm sorry about shouting just now." They had reached Sugarfoot's stall. "Now, what seems to be the problem?"

"Problem?" Kate looked up. "There's no problem."

"I told Ted how you were having problems tacking up," Izzy said, widening her eyes and willing her friend to understand. Kate did.

"I-I mean... I don't have a problem any *more*. Sugarfoot's calmed down and—"

"So you don't need help?" Ted said. "Great. I don't know... You two girls." He shrugged. "I'll see you both at the oval then."

"Yes, fine," Izzy said.

As soon as Ted walked away, Kate turned to her friend. "What's going on, Izzy?"

And Izzy let everything flood out – hearing Ted's conversation, how he had discovered her, how he'd tried to be friendly afterwards – and then she repeated his exact words from the phone call, finishing on the part about killing Seattle Surprise.

"Kill her?" Kate gasped.

"He's going to!" Izzy almost wailed.

"Are you sure you heard right, Izzy?" Kate insisted. "What *exactly* did he say?"

"*Exactly* what I just told you," said Izzy crossly. "If you don't believe me, then—"

"Of course I believe you," Kate interrupted. "But what are we going to do now?"

Chapter 12

Drastic Measures

"Your cell phone is ringing in the kitchen, Izzy," Courtney said that evening. "I saw it was Paula." She frowned. "Don't let Mom know she's calling. Mom's still mad about the other night."

"Oh right... Thanks." Quickly, Izzy hurried out into the kitchen and picked up her phone. "Hello Paula? Thank goodness you've called," she whispered.

"What's happened?" Paula asked quickly.

"I can't explain now, but it's definitely Ted who's doping the horses. I heard him on the phone. And I can't believe it but he said he's going to kill Seattle!"

Paula was quiet.

"Are you still there? What should we do?"

"I'm here," she breathed. "You have to tell Sally. Tell her everything."

"Yes, of course. We can't do anything else."

"Do you want me to come over?" Paula offered.

"No, I don't think so," said Izzy, thinking how angry Sally still was with Paula for bringing them back so late. "I'd better go," she said. "But don't worry. I'll make sure Sally knows."

Izzy finished the call and slipped her mobile in her pocket. Somehow, she had to summon up the courage to tell Sally that her trusted stable manager was the one doping the horses.

"Now? You think I should tell her now?" Izzy asked Kate the following day. She was riding Prince around the jumping paddock.

"Well, you did chicken out of it last night and now seems as good a time as any," Kate answered, cantering Garnet in a neat circle.

"One more time around," said Izzy, turning Prince towards the course once more. They went flying over every jump, clearing each fence easily.

"Wow, Izzy, that was really fast." Kate smiled.

"Stress can help you achieve miracles, obviously," Izzy said, jumping down and leading Prince off by the reins. "Wish me luck."

"I'm coming with you," said Kate.

"Thanks. I thought you'd never offer," her friend replied with a grin.

The two girls led the horses back into the yard.

"Hi," Sally waved. She was hosing down Tobago Bay. "How did you do?"

"Really good, thanks," Izzy said, feeling butterflies in her stomach. It was now or never. "Sally, could we have a word with you?"

"Can it wait?" Sally asked. "I'm in kind of a rush right now – especially with Ted going away."

"Ted's going away?" Izzy glanced at Kate. This changed everything. How could he dope Seattle if he wasn't even going to be around?

"Why the surprise?" Sally said, with a grin. "He is allowed to leave the farm sometimes you know!"

"Um, it just seems strange to take a break with Seattle's race so soon."

"That's his business," said Sally firmly.

Izzy didn't know what to say, so many thoughts were crowding her mind.

"Look, I've got to get going, girls, and you have two ponies to rub down," Sally said, as she turned back to Tobago Bay.

The girls led Prince and Garnet away, gloomily.

"I didn't feel I could say anything after all that," said Izzy.

"No, we could hardly tell her that we think Ted's going to dope Seattle when he's not even going to be here. Where do you think he's going?"

"Who knows?" said Izzy. "But it gives him the perfect alibi, doesn't it? I wouldn't be surprised if he didn't try to sneak into the stable yard at night, like we did at Joe Hagan's, when there's no one around."

She paused, her brow furrowed. It was her 'thinking' face, Kate knew. "We're going to have to guard Seattle in the nights before her race. The security guard can't be everywhere."

"But Sally would never let us do that," Kate said.

"No, she wouldn't, so we're not going to tell her," said Izzy. "We'll stay in Seattle's stable without her knowing about it. It's the only way we can be sure Seattle will be safe."

"But don't you think we should at least tell Megan and Courtney?" asked Kate.

"We can't. You know how loyal they are to Ted," said Izzy.

Kate started to say something and stopped. Izzy was right. Besides, the fewer people who got involved right now, the better.

Chapter 13

Night Watch

Guarding Seattle became a full-time job for Kate and Izzy, and they were proud of themselves. As they set off for their final watch before the race, nothing had happened to her under their protection.

The moon was high in the sky as they made their way through the trees. They waited until the security guard had passed the entrance to the yard, avoided the light sensors and went into the barn. The little grey mare was lying in the straw, but was not yet asleep. She gave a little nicker and got up.

"Shhh, hush now, it's all right, Seattle." Izzy

stroked the pony gently and turned to Kate. "Once she's settled, we'll go in and bed down with her."

"I'm sure that if anything was going to happen to Seattle, it would have happened by now," said Kate, watching the horse lie down again.

Seattle's stall was lit by the little window at the back, and soon pale moonlight flooded in across the floor, illuminating the beautiful, sleeping horse.

"We're going to be exhausted by the morning," Kate said, yawning, "but it'll be worth it."

The two girls sat in the dark, whispering. They knew they'd get bored, but they hadn't realized how tired they would get, too. Within half an hour, Kate was fast asleep.

Izzy sighed. Now she had to be even more alert, but she was so tired... Her eyelids were closing when she thought she heard a grating noise. Had she imagined it? Or dreamt it? No, there it was again. Someone was opening the iron door of the barn.

Izzy froze. "Kate," she hissed, shaking her friend.

Kate sat up. "Sorry... must have fallen asleep."

"Listen! Can you hear something?" Izzy murmured. They both listened. Silence.

"It's nothing, Izzy," Kate said. "You must be imagining it. You know, I think we should—"

The sound echoed around the barn once more.

"Oh my goodness, Izzy! What do we do now?"

"I'm going to confront him," Izzy said, jumping to her feet. "Ted?" she cried. "Is that you?"

It was silent for a moment, but Izzy could definitely make out a shadowy figure in the barn.

"Ted?" she called again, less sure.

In a split second, the figure was gone, racing from the barn.

Izzy sprinted across the yard, past the tack room and over the gate into the dark paddocks beyond. He was getting away! Her lungs felt as though they would burst, she was panting so hard, but she kept on running, using every ounce of strength. It was hopeless. Whoever it was vanished into the darkness.

Wearily she walked across the paddocks. Kate and the security guard rushed towards her.

"Izzy, thank goodness you're all right. You shouldn't have run off like that." Kate hugged her friend tight.

"I'm fine," Izzy said, embarrassed. "He was too fast for me, that's all."

"He's long gone now," the security guard said, looking worried. "Did you get a good look at him?"

"No, not really. I couldn't see much in the dark."

Izzy saw Sally coming through the archway into the yard, closely followed by Courtney and Megan.

"What's going on?" Sally asked, her eyes wide, her hair tousled from sleep.

"Someone was trying to get into Seattle's stable," the security guard told her. "Though how they got into the grounds is a mystery to me. These girls caught him going into the barn."

"But Seattle? Is Seattle all right? Izzy, Kate, tell me what happened." Sally looked alarmed.

"Seattle's fine," Izzy said quickly.

"Oh thank goodness. But what on earth were you doing out here at night?"

"We were, well, we were sleeping in Seattle's stable," Izzy burst out in a rush. "We were worried about her." Izzy waited for Sally to be angry.

Instead, she hugged them both. "Oh, you silly girls. You put yourselves in real danger. Enough's enough." Sally covered her face in her hands, and started to cry. "We can't go on like this. I should never have let Ted go. We need him here."

Kate and Izzy looked at each other. Should they say something now? But when Sally headed off, they knew another chance was gone.

They followed her into the barn to check on Seattle. The little grey mare was sleeping soundly.

"She's fine," said Sally, softly. She turned to the security guard. "But why weren't you guarding the barn?" she demanded.

"Ma'am, you told me to patrol the grounds," he replied gruffly.

"Yes, well, from now until morning I want you to stand outside this barn. I'll call the police as soon as I can tomorrow. Now, let's get some sleep."

Chapter 14

Clevedon Park

No one said much over breakfast the next morning, but when Courtney got up from the table, she turned on Izzy.

"We're really mad at you," she said, angrily. "Why didn't you include us in your plans? We trusted you... Why couldn't you trust us?"

Izzy didn't know what to say. How could she tell them that they'd decided not to because of how they felt about Ted? Luckily, Sally came into the room at that moment, and she could change the subject.

"Morning! Did Seattle get off to the track all

right?" she asked, with fake cheeriness.

"Fine," Sally answered.

"She will be safe, won't she?" said Courtney, concern in her voice.

"Of course she will," said Sally. "Hank Brewer's been driving for us for years. He won't let her out of his sight. I would have liked to have gone in the trailer with her, but with Ted away there's no one else to see to the other horses here. We'll get to the track by noon," Sally added wearily. "Look Izzy, I know that you must have gone over this many times already, but is there anything you can remember about the man you saw?"

"Well..." Izzy faltered. "It was so dark, I couldn't really see. He wasn't very tall... that's about it."

Sally sighed. "Well, if anything should come to you, anything at all, tell us. I know that it's hard, but anything you remember could hold the key to it all."

"I know. Of course I will," said Izzy. If only she could say she'd definitely seen Ted... but she couldn't.

"Don't worry." Sally patted her on the shoulder.

"Let's get over to the yard and start mucking out."

"Sally," Izzy said, hesitating. The time to say something about Ted had to be now.

"Yes?" Sally turned back.

"It's just something that Kate and I have been thinking..."

"Go on."

"W-well," Izzy stammered. "We were wondering – I mean – where's Ted at the moment?"

"Ted?" Sally looked surprised. "What's that got to do with anything? Surely you don't think he's our night-time intruder?" She laughed.

"Well..." Izzy hesitated.

Sally stared at her. "You *are* kidding?"

"We did think it was a little strange that he's gone away for a few days." Kate stepped in. "I mean, it's Seattle's big race today..." This was so awkward, but there was no nice way of putting it. "Ted knows the farm from back to front. It would be easy for him to slip past the security guard, and he's been around all the other times when the horses were doped and—"

"It's not Ted," Sally interrupted.

"But how can you be sure?" asked Kate.

"I just am," Sally said, firmly. "Now, come on. We've got work to do." And with that, she left the room, followed by her daughters.

Kate turned to Izzy. "So that's it. We've blown it. No one is ever going to believe us about Ted now. He's going to get away with it all."

It was midday when Sally turned into the car park at Clevedon Park Racetrack, and the place was already busy. Izzy and Kate followed Sally through the turnstiles, but they were not looking forward to the day any more. They were upset, worried about Seattle, and the twins were being really unfriendly.

Sally handed everyone their badges as they stopped in front of a stunning bronze statue of a horse. Clevedon Park was nothing like the racecourses that Izzy and Kate had been to in England. They'd only been National Hunt racing, and that was in the winter. Today, the sun was blazing and a band was striking up. It was more like a wonderful horse-filled festival.

"Seattle's not running until the third race, so I'm going to check on her," Sally told them. "Why don't you all go and soak up the atmosphere? We'll meet over there just before Seattle's race." She pointed to a spot near the grandstand.

All four girls nodded. Sally walked away and an awkward silence followed.

"I guess that's the winning post then?" Izzy said finally, pointing to the red and white pole in front of the manicured lawns.

"Yeah, well, it's called the wire over here, but it's the same thing," said Courtney. "Should we go and check out the competition?"

Izzy and Kate trailed after Courtney and Megan through a white-railed gate to where a man was checking entry tickets.

Everywhere they looked, grooms were leading sheeted horses, people were running around and camera crews were wheeling equipment and holding microphones, preparing for the live TV coverage.

Suddenly, Courtney and Megan ducked under the railings. "Okay, we're going to find Seattle. Meet you to the right of the grandstand in half an hour."

"Good idea," said Izzy. It would be nice to have some time away from the twins, to cool off a bit.

"We've totally ruined things with Courtney and Megan now," Kate said.

"Yeah, think so," Izzy answered. "Hey, look over there. Isn't that Paula?"

"Where?" Kate squinted into the sun and saw Paula, threading her way through the crowd. They hadn't spoken to their friend since that last phone conversation, when she had urged Izzy to tell Sally their suspicions. Surely they should tell her everything that had happened since?

"Come on," Izzy said. "Let's go and see her."

"Paula..." Kate called breathlessly, as they darted through the crowds as fast as they could, heading for their vanishing friend. "Paula!"

It looked at first as though they'd never catch her. There were just too many people, and she was moving too fast. Then she looked back, saw them and stopped.

"Oh, it's you guys. What are you two doing here?" she said, with a frown.

"It's Seattle's big race – remember?" Izzy said.

"Oh yes, so it is. Let's hope she runs well today." Paula smiled, but her manner was far from friendly. "Look, I'm busy. What was it you wanted?"

"Well, nothing really – just to say hello," Izzy said, puzzled by Paula's attitude. "And to tell you what's been going on at Graytops."

"There was an intruder at the farm last night," said Kate. "We started to tell Sally that we thought it could be Ted, but she said it couldn't possibly be."

"Did you tell her you'd seen his face?" asked Paula.

"Well no, because we didn't see it," Izzy said.

"Hmm, you should have told her about Ted from the beginning, when I told you to – when we found that sticky note."

"Yes, well, you may be right, but it was tricky," said Izzy uncomfortably. This was not going well.

She looked closely at Paula, whose face was covered with drops of sweat. "Are you feeling all right?"

"I'm fine," Paula snapped, but she didn't look it.

"Seattle will be safe today anyway, because Ted's not around," Kate said.

"*Safe?*" Paula sneered. "Well, if she is, it won't be because of you two!"

Izzy and Kate were so shocked by this surprise outburst, they stared at her in silence.

"Ted may not be here, but Joe Hagan is," Paula went on. "It'll be your fault if Seattle's found with benzocaine in her system, just like the last horse..."

"Hey, Paula, calm down," said Kate. This was getting out of hand.

"Give me a break! I've got better things to do with my time than argue with you two jerks. Some of us have work to do."

And she disappeared into the crowd.

"What was that about?" Kate looked bewildered.

"Do you think she's not feeling well? Did you see the way she was sweating?" Izzy answered.

"Yes, her fringe was plastered to her face," Kate said. "But to speak to us like that. So rude... I thought she was our friend."

Izzy snorted. "We might be younger than her but she didn't need to call us 'jerks'. And what exactly did she mean, when she said it would be our fault if Seattle was found with benzo—" She stopped short. "Benzocaine!"

"But no one's supposed to know about that drug," Kate said, her eyes wide. "No one outside the family. Oh, Izzy..."

All the blood seemed to drain from Izzy's face. "Kate, we've been barking up completely the wrong tree. We've got to get to Seattle – NOW!"

Chapter 15

A Nasty Discovery

It seemed to take Izzy and Kate forever to push their way through the crowds... through the gate... past the parade ring... until, out of breath, they finally reached the track that led down to the stables.

"Hey you two – you can't go down there," a security guard called after them, but there was no stopping them. Swerving past horses and riders, they charged towards Seattle's stable.

"There's Sally!" Izzy said, panting.

"Sally... Sally!" yelled Kate.

"What in the world...?"

"No... time... to... explain," Izzy managed to say. "Where's Seattle?"

"She's in that stall, with Paula," Sally said. "What's all this about?"

Izzy and Kate didn't stop to reply. They reached Seattle's box just in time to see their friend holding a syringe of pale liquid up in front of her, her hair glowing beneath the light bulb that was swinging above her head.

"Paula, STOP!" Izzy cried.

"Izzy, Kate? What are you two doing here?" She seemed more friendly than a few minutes ago, but she had swiftly put her hand behind her back.

"What's in your hand?" Izzy stepped into the stall.

"Hand?" Paula looked surprised and laughed.

"We know you've got a syringe, Paula. You've just been using us, telling us all that nonsense about Ted being the guilty one when it was YOU!"

And now, as Paula glared at her, Izzy could see no warmth in her eyes at all.

"You were about to inject Seattle with something,

weren't you?" Kate joined in.

"And you think you're going to stop me?" Paula said coldly. "No way!"

"Drop that, Paula." Sally's shocked face appeared at the door to the stable. Carefully, she walked between Izzy and Kate and into the stall. Courtney and Megan stood close behind her, their eyes blazing with anger.

Seattle Surprise lashed out with her hind legs against the rear of the stall, but Paula didn't move a muscle. "I'm not dropping anything – not for anyone..." she hissed. "I have to do this."

Paula's arm lunged forward to jab Seattle when Courtney suddenly flung herself forward, sending the syringe flying into the air. As the two girls wrestled, the syringe clattered to the floor. Megan immediately stamped on it, shattering it into a million pieces.

Paula stared at her in disbelief. "You... you've messed up everything," she cried, burying her head in her hands. Then, all they heard were her awful, racking sobs as she slumped to the floor.

Sally ignored her, being more worried about calming Seattle. "Megan, Courtney. Call security."

The twins raced off, to reappear a couple of minutes later with two security men.

"I'm Sally Bryant," Sally told them, her voice trembling. "This girl has just tried to dope my horse, Seattle Surprise. Would you take her away?"

The men grabbed Paula's hands. Izzy would never forget the crumpled look on Paula's face as she was led out of the stables...

At three o'clock, the gates slammed open and the horses were away in the Gresham Maiden Stakes.

Speeding cleanly out of the stalls, Seattle Surprise jostled with the other horses until finally she settled mid-field. Izzy listened to the commentator, hardly daring to breathe.

"And it's Silver Dollar who's kicked clear of the pack by two lengths. Racing quickly in the red is Sprightly Lad, Night Clown is tucked in behind these in third, and then Seattle Surprise is on the rails in fourth." The other names, Izzy didn't even listen to. She only wanted to know about one horse in this race.

"She's sitting nicely," Courtney murmured as the horses raced through the clubhouse turn.

Izzy looked at Sally. Her knuckles were as white as chalk as she gripped the sides of her binoculars. Silver Dollar was setting a cracking pace, stretching the pack out, but Seattle wasn't far off the lead.

"They're through the first furlong," announced the commentator. "Serendipity is the back marker of the field, but it's Silver Dollar who has increased his margin to three lengths from Sprightly Lad."

"Don't let them run away with you, Seattle Surprise," Izzy whispered.

"And it's Silver Dollar on the inside, Sprightly Lad in second and Night Clown is back in third," the commentator called. "Seattle Surprise is in fourth, and coming very fast in the pink sleeves is River Boy and then it's half a length back to Field of Dreams.

They're racing very quickly now. Making headway is Seattle Surprise."

"Come on, Seattle," Izzy and Kate cried excitedly.

"It's still Silver Dollar out in front, half a length back is Sprightly Lad. Night Clown has dropped away now, and Seattle Surprise is chasing along in third. Moving up on the outside are River Boy and Field of Dreams."

"Don't get boxed in," Kate murmured in dismay as she realized the race was nearing the end and that there were two horses closing up on Seattle's outside.

"And it's Silver Dollar and Sprightly Lad who have been joined by River Boy. Field of Dreams is on the outside of these and Seattle Surprise is trying to find an opening, but there's nowhere for her to go..."

The horses ran around the far turn.

"Come on, Seattle," Courtney whispered. "You can find a way through."

The crowd started cheering and Izzy gripped Kate's shoulder as she watched the little grey mare fighting for her ground. There could only be some three furlongs left. It looked an impossible task. She wasn't going to do it.

"But look, Seattle Surprise is pulling wide," the commentator cried with excitement. "Field of Dreams has dropped away, so has River Boy, and Seattle Surprise is moving up into third – she's only some three lengths off the lead. And it's Sprightly Lad and Silver Dollar, racing neck and neck, with Seattle Surprise coming up to challenge them both."

The four girls could hardly bear to watch. Seattle was gaining ground all the time but the winning line was getting closer and closer.

"Sprightly Lad has the edge, Silver Dollar is fading, and it's Seattle Surprise who is challenging his lead."

"Come on Seattle!" Izzy and Kate were jumping up and down.

"And what a remarkable recovery – it's Seattle Surprise and Sprightly Lad, racing neck and neck... too close to call! Stand by for the photo!"

The horses flashed past the winning post in a flurry of legs, manes, tails and shouting.

"Did she get it?" Izzy and Kate said excitedly. They turned around, but Sally had disappeared. Courtney and Megan were looking worried.

"*Did* she get it?" Courtney repeated.

"I'm not sure." Izzy felt nervous. "But did you see the way she found that extra spurt of speed to catch the leaders? She came from nowhere. Amazing."

The girls tore across the grass to the winner's enclosure to watch Seattle Surprise being led off the track. Seattle's flanks were glistening with sweat, but her ears were pricked. And then the results of the photo-finish were announced:

"Number 10, Seattle Surprise..."

Izzy and Kate didn't listen to the rest. They could hardly hear themselves speak as they jumped up and down, whooping with delight. They turned to Courtney and Megan, who looked ecstatic as they all linked arms and cheered together.

"One thing's for sure," Izzy grinned. "There won't be any problems when the results of the drugs test comes back. We know she's won on merit alone."

Chapter 16

All is Revealed

"To think that we came so close to losing everything." Doug Bryant stood looking out over the paddocks at Graytops, surrounded by his family, his loyal stable manager and Kate and Izzy.

The girls had just met him for the first time, and were immediately impressed by his open, honest face. "It's great to be back," he murmured, smiling as he watched the yearlings chasing each other.

"Everything's going to be all right now, Doug." Sally rested her hand on his shoulder. "This whole nightmare is over."

It had only been yesterday that Seattle Surprise had won her race and Paula had confessed to her involvement in the doping, but to Izzy and Kate, it already felt like a lifetime ago.

"I never imagined for a moment that Paula could be behind it," Sally said, shaking her head. "She was always a little strange, and that story she made up about saving Seattle from colic... Crazy... But to actually try to ruin us? Why?"

"I don't think any of us could have imagined what she was up to," Doug said. "How could we have known how much she hated our family? I would never have guessed that Hal was her father."

"Me neither," Sally said, thoughtfully. "I certainly wouldn't have recognized her from when he was our stable manager. She was just a little girl back then."

Izzy and Kate were completely baffled and even Courtney and Megan were looking at their parents with puzzled expressions, obviously waiting for a fuller explanation.

"Do you remember Hal, girls?" Doug said. "You

may not. He was our stable manager when you were barely more than toddlers. We had to fire him when we realized he was stealing from us. He'd started to drink too much when his marriage broke down and then Paula's younger sister was killed in a horrific car crash. He just fell apart, poor guy. I guess Paula needed someone to blame for all that misery. I feel pretty sorry for her. She certainly hasn't had the easiest of lives."

"Sorry?" Courtney burst out. "How can you feel sorry for her after everything she's done? She doped our horses *and* she broke into Graytops!"

The other three girls nodded their agreement.

"Paula is ill, Courtney. She needs professional help," Doug said firmly. "Hopefully, she'll get some now. Stress and grief can make you do all sorts of terrible things. All I want is for Graytops to get back to normal. Now that everyone knows I wasn't doping the horses and my suspension has been lifted, that shouldn't take too long. I think we have a busy future ahead – and it's all thanks to Izzy and Kate."

Izzy and Kate squirmed. It was time for the truth. They still hadn't told the Bryants about their late night visit to Joe Hagan's farm with Paula. This was not going to be easy.

"Um... Doug and Sally, we've got a confession to make," Izzy began. "We were really taken in by Paula. We had no clue what she was up to until the very last minute. As you know, Sally, we thought the culprit was Ted."

"Me?" Ted exclaimed, clearly shocked.

"That's what Paula wanted us to believe," Izzy added hurriedly. "I know it sounds crazy but she convinced us you were working for Joe Hagan."

"Joe Hagan? But what's he got to do with any of this?" Doug asked.

Kate looked embarrassed. "It just seemed too much of a coincidence to us that Joe Hagan's horses came in second on both occasions."

"And then when we found out that Joe had Ted's phone number, it convinced us that Joe must be using Ted to do his dirty work." Now Izzy looked sheepish. Even as she said it, she heard how feeble it sounded.

"But Joe's just a friend. We've worked in the business for years," said Ted. "There wasn't anything sinister about him having my cell phone number."

"Yes, we realize that now," Kate said, in a rather subdued voice.

"It seems as if we have a case of an over-active imagination here," joked Sally, trying to defuse the situation. "Luckily, no damage has been done."

But there was still something bothering Izzy: Ted's telephone conversation, the one she had overheard in the office, when she had been convinced he was planning to kill Seattle Surprise.

"I'll fight you every step of the way... I can't get you that kind of money... But that would kill her!"

What had that all been about, if it wasn't about Seattle Surprise?

"Well, I did overhear Ted saying something on the phone, which made us suspicious too," she said, nervously.

"You mean the day I caught you spying on me?" Ted spluttered. "See what happens when you snoop on people..."

"Yes, but... but... I wasn't sn-nooping on you," Izzy stammered.

"I was talking to my ex-wife," Ted explained. "The last couple of months haven't been the easiest for me." He sighed. "I'm getting divorced and we've had custody hearings for my daughter. My wife wanted to take her to live in New York State."

Izzy and Kate gulped. There was nothing to say, apart from, "Sorry."

"Well, it's all sorted now," said Ted, clearing his throat. "She's staying here."

"She is?" Courtney and Megan cried.

"Yeah." Ted's face relaxed into his unique, crooked smile. "I think my ex-wife has realized that Andrea needs her father as much as I need her." He looked at Izzy and Kate. "I suppose I haven't been very nice to you since you got here, with the stress of it all. I'm sorry too. Let's put it behind us, eh?"

"Let's," they said, in unison.

"So everything turned out okay," Courtney said, putting an arm around each of her parents.

"Yes, but I'm so sorry all this has been going on while you've been out here, girls. It hasn't been a vacation at all for you, has it?" Sally said.

"But we've had a great time, haven't we, Kate?" Izzy said. "And it's certainly been, well, different." She grinned. "We'll never forget our time here at Graytops, that's for sure."

"You've both been fantastic," said Doug. "I can't thank you enough for all your hard work."

"You know we'll miss you when you're gone," Courtney said. "It'll be kinda quiet on the farm. Maybe you could come and stay some other time?"

"Love to, if you promise not to make us work like slaves!" said Izzy, with a laugh.

"It's a deal." Megan laughed too. "But first things first – we've got a summer trip to Sandy Lane to look forward to next year."

"A quiet, chilled out one, I hope," said Courtney.

"Quiet? Hmm..." Izzy replied.

Perhaps anything would seem 'quiet' after the dramas of that summer at Graytops, but 'chilled out'? No, Sandy Lane was never that – there was always far too much going on.

"Well, we'll do our best to keep it peaceful for you," said Izzy, winking at Kate. "But we're not making any promises..."

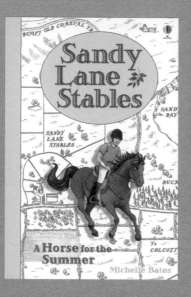

A Horse for the Summer

Michelle Bates

Ride by Moonlight

Michelle Bates

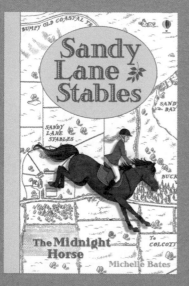

The Midnight Horse

Michelle Bates

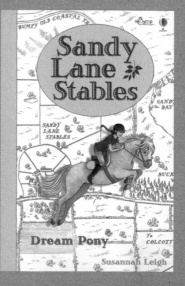

Dream Pony

Susannah Leigh